Andi Saddles Up

Circle C Stepping Stones

Andi Saddles Up
Andi Under the Big Top
Andi Lassos Trouble
Andi to the Rescue
Andi Dreams of Gold
Andi Far from Home

Circle C Stepping Stones #1

Andi Saddles Up

Susan K. Marlow

Kregel
Publications

Andi Saddles Up
© 2017 by Susan K. Marlow

Illustrations © 2017 by Leslie Gammelgaard

Published by Kregel Publications, a division of Kregel, Inc., 2450 Oak Industrial Dr. NE, Grand Rapids, MI 49505.

ISBN 978-0-8254-4430-2

Printed in the United States of America
17 18 19 20 21 22 23 24 25 26 / 5 4 3 2 1

Contents

New Words. 7

1. Birthday Wish 9
2. Birthday Interruption 17
3. Horse and Rider 25
4. No Means No 33
5. Special Spot. 39
6. New Friend 47
7. Surprises 55
8. Show-Offs 65
9. Trouble 73
10. The Accident 81
11. Painful Lesson. 89
12. Good Neighbors 95

History Fun:
Sheep and Cattle Wars 103

New Words

alfalfa—the best kind of hay for horses and cattle

cinch—(*verb*) to fasten tightly; (*noun*) the wide strap that goes under a horse's belly and holds the saddle in place

conchos—silver decorations on a saddle

doughball—a small lump of dough used as bait for fishing

filly—a young female horse

palomino—a golden-colored horse with a white- or cream-colored mane and tail

ranch hand—someone who works for the owner of a ranch; also called a "cowhand"

range—wide-open, natural grazing land for horses, cattle, and sheep

saddle broke—a horse that has been trained to carry a rider

stringer—a line that holds fish to keep them alive in water after being caught

tack—equipment used on horses: saddles, stirrups, bridles, halters, and reins

tack up—to prepare a horse for riding with saddle, reins, and other tack

whicker—a soft neigh or whinny

woolgathering—daydreaming

⚕ CHAPTER 1 ⚕

Birthday Wish

Spring 1877

"Today is the day," Andi Carter chanted in a sing-song voice. "Today is the day . . ." She paused, thinking hard. Then she burst out, "Oh, how I love the month of May!"

She ran a brush along the back of her palomino filly. "Did you hear that, Taffy? My verse rhymes. Miss Hall is teaching us poetry in school." Andi wrinkled her forehead. "I never found much use for it before today."

Taffy tugged a wisp of hay from her feeder and turned her large, dark eyes on Andi. She chewed but made no other sound.

"Don't you *know*?" Andi jumped down from the

overturned bucket she always used to reach Taffy's back. She tossed aside her brush and grabbed Taffy's golden head with both hands. "It's our birthday today. Yours and mine. You're three and I'm nine."

Another rhyme! She giggled. "Remember?"

Taffy didn't nicker. She didn't snort or whinny. Instead, she jerked her head out of Andi's grasp and grabbed more hay.

Chomp, chomp, chomp.

Did Taffy ever think of anything besides eating her sweet alfalfa?

"You should be more excited about this," Andi said. "I've waited three whole years to finally be able to ride you whenever I want." She pulled her filly's head down and whispered in her ear. "With your own saddle. You and me. Horse and rider at last."

Andi had ridden Taffy bareback plenty of times during the past year. But she always rode under the watchful eye of her brother Chad, the ranch boss. He was *her* boss too, when it came to training Taffy.

"Patience, little sister," Chad said much too often for Andi's liking. "Taffy will have a saddle on her back soon enough."

Soon enough always seemed like such a long way off. "But not anymore," Andi said happily. She rubbed Taffy's golden nose. "Today is the day!"

Tingles raced up and down Andi's arms. She would ride Taffy with her very own saddle!

Up till now, Andi could ride almost any horse on the Circle C ranch. A ranch hand stood ready to help her lift a heavy saddle and cinch it on Patches, the paint horse, or Pal, the bay. She only had to ask.

But those saddles were meant for grown-up cowhands. Andi always slid around on those big, full-sized seats.

She could also ride her pony, Coco. Andi could saddle Coco all by herself anytime she wanted—which wasn't very often. Riding Coco wasn't much fun with or without a saddle. He was too old and too tired. He trotted slower than a muddy creek in summer.

And he never, *ever* galloped.

Andi looked at Coco's small saddle. It hung over the stall railing just across the walkway. She sighed. Was there ever a saddle more worn out? Or cracked? Or one that showed more slash marks than this scraggly piece of tack?

Big brother Chad was sure handy with a knife, even when he was a little boy. He'd scratched up the saddle, but the words were still visible. Andi read them out loud and made a face.

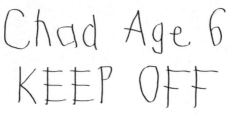

Chad Age 6
KEEP OFF

Andi turned her back on Coco's saddle. She had never thought of it as her own. Not with Chad's name gouged into it. Grown-up brothers Justin, Chad, and Mitch had used that old thing. Big sister Melinda had used it too.

And me.

No more. Taffy was too pretty to lug around a shabby piece of leather on her golden back.

"Besides," Andi said, "the cinch would never fit around your belly." She giggled. "Especially the way you've been eating these days."

Taffy's ears pricked up. She whickered and shook her creamy mane. Then she stamped her foot. The straw bedding rustled.

Andi laughed. "I knew you would agree."

"Agree about what?"

Chad's voice pulled Andi around. "Taffy and I agree that she will never wear that old thing." She jabbed her finger at Coco's saddle.

Chad joined Andi in the stall. He raised his eyebrows at her. "Really? Do you plan on riding Taffy bareback all the time? Where will you keep your lasso?"

Andi's mouth dropped wide open. She would ride Taffy with a saddle, of course! But with a saddle all her own. *Not* with a hand-me-down one.

Before Andi could tell Chad what she was thinking, he said, "Or will you dig around in the tack room for a different saddle?" He shook his head. "You aren't strong enough to lift any of those."

"But—"

Chad waved his hand toward Coco's saddle. "It appears to me that, for now, this saddle is more your size. I can rig a longer cinch to fit around Taffy's belly."

Plunk! Andi's heart dropped like a stone into her stomach.

Was Chad teasing her? How could he not know Andi wanted a saddle for her birthday? She had given her family about a million hints during the past month.

She peered into Chad's bright-blue eyes. No teasing sparkles laughed back at her. He looked serious, like he knew best.

This is terrible. My worst birthday ever.

Tears watered Andi's eyes, but she would not cry. Chad didn't know everything. He would probably be surprised when he saw a new saddle sitting in Andi's chair at breakfast. A saddle was too big to hide and too lumpy to wrap.

"It's Taffy's birthday today too, Chad," she said, blinking hard. "Didn't you remember?"

"Of course I remembered." He rubbed the white blaze on Taffy's nose. "Happy birthday, girl."

Andi's spirits rose a little at her brother's cheerful words. For three years, he had helped her train Taffy.

For three years, Andi had taken extra good care of Coco—just to show Chad she was old enough to train and take care of Taffy.

As Taffy grew stronger, Chad let Andi ride her. What happy days those were! The best news of all? Chad and Mother agreed that when Andi turned nine, she could ride Taffy whenever she wanted.

To Andi, that meant a saddle of her own.

Weeks ago, Andi had picked out the perfect saddle. Every day after school, her oldest and favorite brother, Justin, drove Andi and Melinda home in the buggy. Every day she begged him to pass by Beckman's saddle shop.

"That one right there in the window," she said, pointing. "The one with the swirly designs and the pretty silver conchos. I'm sure it's just my size."

Melinda always rolled her eyes, and Justin always nodded. But neither ever said a word. Andi knew her sister was tired of hearing about saddles, but—

"Andi!"

She jumped. "What?"

Chad tugged one of her long dark braids. "I came to get you for breakfast, birthday girl. Let's go inside."

Andi pushed her worried thoughts aside. It was time for breakfast—her birthday breakfast.

And hopefully a birthday saddle.

CHAPTER 2

Birthday Interruption

Andi skipped behind Chad all the way across the yard. The rising sun peeked over the mountains, promising a fair day. Best of all, it was a Saturday.

No school on my birthday!

Andi's joy soared higher than the lone hawk circling way above her head. She ducked around Chad and clattered up the porch steps. A quick scrub at the kitchen pump and she was ready for breakfast.

Her special birthday breakfast.

Only on birthdays did Mother and their housekeeper, Luisa, take the time and trouble to heat up the heavy cast-iron waffle maker. It sat on the cookstove now. Steam curled up from around its edges. A delicious waffle aroma filled the kitchen.

Andi's mouth watered. She burst into the dining room, eager to taste that first sweet bite.

"Happy birthday, Andi!" her family called out.

Andi's gaze immediately flew to her place at the table. A waffle rested on her plate, fresh and hot, with a big pat of butter on top. A cup of steaming chocolate sat beside it. Everything Andi had asked for. Everything but . . .

She hurried over to her chair. It was empty. Five colorfully wrapped packages surrounded her breakfast plate. One was big, but not big enough to hold a saddle. Not by a long shot.

Andi lifted the tablecloth, bent over, and peeked under the table. No saddle lay hidden there. Only four pairs of feet and legs. Five when Chad sat down.

"What are you doing, Andrea?"

Andi dropped the tablecloth and stood up. "Nothing, Mother." She glanced at the dining room corner, just in case. No saddle there either.

She sighed, but kept it to herself. Chad had not been teasing after all. Apparently, Andi was not old enough for a saddle of her own. *Please, God, don't let Mother see how disappointed I am.*

Andi was nine years old today, which sounded so much more grown-up than eight. She would be thankful for her birthday breakfast and for whatever the pretty packages held. She put a smile on her face and sat down.

Justin asked the blessing.

When he said "amen," Andi picked up the pitcher and dumped syrup until it flooded her plate. The waffle tasted good, but some of the sunshine had gone out of her birthday. She sipped her chocolate and thought hard about a new saddle.

The day was just beginning. Mother would bake Andi's birthday cake this afternoon. Surprises sometimes happened later in the day. Not often, but it was possible. Maybe it wasn't too late to hope for a saddle.

She finished her waffle, drank the last chocolaty drops in her cup, and looked around. Everybody else was finished too. They were waiting for Andi.

Luisa took away Andi's plate and cup. Fourteen-year-old Melinda plunked a small, ribbon-tied package in front of the birthday girl. "Open mine first. I picked it out specially for you."

Andi tore away the wrappings. A bright red-and-black square of cloth fell out. "A bandana!"

"It's not very ladylike," Melinda said. She shrugged. "But I knew you'd like it better than an embroidered hankie."

"I do." Andi reached over and hugged her sister. "Thank you."

The other gifts made Andi gasp with delight. A beautiful new halter for Taffy. A bridle and shiny bit. Reins. Even a new hoof pick.

"Don't lose this one," Mitch said, laughing.

Everybody knew Andi went through hoof picks like Taffy went through grain.

Andi neatly laid out her gifts on the table to admire them. She had everything she needed so she and Taffy could be horse and rider. Everything except a—

Bang, bang, bang!

Andi jumped in her seat. So did Melinda.

Chad scowled. "Who would beat on our front door first thing in the morning?"

"It could be trouble out on the range," Mitch said.

Andi knew better. The ranch hands usually came to the back door.

Bang, bang . . . crash!

Even from the dining room, Andi heard the front door slam against the wall. Someone was not only interrupting her birthday breakfast, but they had barged right into their house!

Andi held her breath. Who would be so rude?

Thumping footsteps drew nearer. A flood of Spanish words followed the footsteps.

Luisa must be very angry to scold the intruder in Spanish, Andi thought. Luisa only scolded Andi in Spanish when she was especially mad at her. Like when Andi slid down the banister railing once too often.

20

A large man suddenly filled the doorway.

Chad sprang from his seat. "Hollister, what are you doing here?"

Luisa pushed past the man. "I am so sorry, *Señor* Chad. He walked right in and demanded to speak to you." She put her hands on her hips and glared at Mr. Hollister.

Andi slid down in her chair. The tall, black-bearded stranger looked mean . . . and angry. He didn't politely take off his hat. His grubby overalls were missing a buckle. And he carried a shotgun in one hand.

"Get your hat off right now, and put that thing down." Chad waved at the shotgun. "What do you want?"

Andi gulped back her surprise. Most of the time, guests at the Circle C ranch were offered coffee and a cheerful "howdy."

Not this time. Chad sounded just as angry as Mr. Hollister looked.

Andi tried to make herself small. She wanted to crawl under the table, but she was too old for that. So she closed her eyes instead and prayed that Mr. Hollister would go away.

For a few seconds, Andi heard nothing. Had God answered her prayer so quickly? Had Mr. Hollister left? Curious, she opened her eyes.

Mr. Hollister still stood in the dining room, eyes

blazing, his hat in his hand. He and Chad stood nose to nose, scowling at each other but not saying a word. Fortunately, his shotgun leaned against the wall.

Then Mr. Hollister began to shout. "Don't you *ever* show up at my place again when I'm not there! You scared the womenfolk and kids half to death." He shook his finger in Chad's face. "That chunk of land is mine now. God changed the creek's course. You can't do nothin' about it, so stay away. You hear me, boy?"

Chad was not a boy. He'd run the ranch since their father had died over three years ago. Standing next to the angry Mr. Hollister, though, Chad looked even younger than his twenty-four years.

"It's not your land," Chad said. "It's two hundred acres of our best grazing land. No sheep are going to chomp it down to the bare roots. Not while *I* own it."

"You don't own it no more," Mr. Hollister yelled.

"Hold on, Chad." Justin pushed back his chair and stood up. "You too, Vince. This boundary disagreement cannot be settled in our dining room. Let's—"

"Sure it can," Mr. Hollister cut in. "It's clear as glass. Spring Creek has always been the boundary between our two places. Spring Creek is *still* the boundary." He grinned, showing a mouthful of broken yellow teeth. "It's just in a different place now."

He plunked his raggedy hat down on his head. "God sent that spring flood, boys. It changed the creek's course. Live with it."

"Vince . . ." Justin tried again.

"Y'all keep away from my place." Mr. Hollister eyed Chad. "I got no problem shootin' trespassers, specially rich ranchers." He turned to Justin. "Or cocky young lawyers."

Mr. Hollister grabbed his shotgun and tipped his hat to Mother. "Sorry, ma'am, for disturbin' your breakfast." He turned on his heel and stomped out of the room.

The front door slammed.

Andi sat up. Her heart pounded. *What a terrible way to start my birthday!*

⊰ CHAPTER 3 ⊱

Horse and Rider

"**W**hat's the matter, sweetheart?"

Mother's quiet question jerked Andi from her thoughts.

"I don't think she liked our early-morning visitor," Melinda said before Andi could answer. "Her face is white."

"I didn't like him *at all*," Andi said in a shaky voice. "He scared me."

"There's no need to be afraid of Mr. Hollister," Justin said. His smiling blue eyes met Andi's.

"But"—Andi gulped—"he said he'd shoot you."

Chad chuckled. "Aw, Andi, don't pay Mr. Hollister any mind. He's just full of bluster."

"What's bluster?" Andi wrinkled her forehead.

Mother smiled. "It means he likes to holler and

throw his weight around, but nothing ever comes of it."

"Ohhh . . ." Andi brightened. She cocked her head and looked at Chad. "Just like you."

Laughter rippled around the table.

Chad turned red, and his mouth dropped open. Then he chuckled again. "You got me there, little sister."

He reached across the table and ruffled Andi's hair. "Speaking of bluster, I reckon I was a bit blustery this morning in the barn." He waved a hand over the spread-out horse tack. "Why don't you go out and see if this all fits on Taffy."

Andi jumped up from her chair. Thoughts of scary Mr. Hollister vanished. "Good idea."

She tied her brand-new bandana around her neck and stuffed the hoof pick in her overalls pocket. Then she gathered up her new bridle and bit, reins, and halter.

"Quite an armful," Mitch said. "Need any help with Taffy?"

Andi shook her head. She knew how to tack up a horse.

"I think we'd better go along with you," Chad said. "Just in case you drop something on the way."

Andi hugged her birthday gifts to her chest. "I won't drop anything." She hurried through the kitchen and out the back door. Her family trailed behind her, even Mother.

When Andi peeked over her shoulder, Justin winked at her.

What's going on?

The morning sun made Andi blink. She crossed the yard toward the barn then stopped short. Taffy was not in her stall. Someone had led her outside and tied her to the railing while Andi was inside eating breakfast.

Not only that, but—

Taffy was wearing a brand-new saddle.

Andi squealed and dropped her armload of horse tack. She dashed over to her palomino filly. "Oh, oh, oh!"

It was not the saddle Andi had seen at the saddle shop. It was better. She ran her fingers over the hand-tooled stars that decorated the saddle's edge. Stars were also carved on the leather above the stirrups.

Then she saw the sparkling silver conchos. They were shaped like stars and matched the designs in the leather. She caught her breath. "Oh, oh, oh!"

Melinda laughed. "Is that all you can say, Andi?"

Andi spun around. Her family stood in a half circle, smiling at her. She threw herself into Mother's arms and then hugged her brothers and sister. "Thank you, thank you! It's perfect. The best saddle in the whole world."

"It's a bit larger than I like for your size," Chad said. "But you won't always be little. You can grow into it."

Andi nodded and raced back to the saddle. By the time she finished admiring it, Mitch had picked up the dropped tack and bridled Taffy.

Everything fit perfectly.

Andi needed no help climbing into her new saddle. It didn't feel too big to her. It felt just right. She took the reins from Mitch and let him adjust the stirrups until they fit just right too.

Justin crossed his arms and let out an admiring whistle. "That's a mighty fine-looking horse and rider we've got on our ranch. Wouldn't you agree, Mother?"

Andi beamed. Horse and rider at last!

"Yes, indeed," Mother replied. Her eyes looked misty. "You are growing up so fast, Andrea."

Why did Mother say that? Andi had been riding horses since she was old enough to sit with Father in the saddle. *Maybe it's because I have my own horse to ride now.* She wished Father could see her. Maybe he was smiling down at her from heaven right this minute.

"Can Taffy and I go riding now, Mother?" she asked. "Please?"

Chad grinned. "She does need to break in that new saddle. I'll get Sky and—"

"You don't have to go with me," Andi said. "I know my way around the ranch. I ride by myself all the time."

"You have ridden Patches or Pal or one of the older

29

horses," Chad said. "But you've never taken a young filly like Taffy out on your own. I want to make sure she has no surprises waiting for you under that new saddle."

"She'd never throw me," Andi said.

"Probably not," Mother agreed with a nod. "But Taffy is young, and so are you."

It was settled.

Andi let out a disappointed breath. "Yes, ma'am."

Once out on the range, Andi's spirits rose. Chad might be bossy, but he was an excellent horseman and trainer. He let Andi do whatever she wanted on Taffy. He even agreed to a short race.

Andi lost.

Taffy was not a very good roping horse either. Andi could lasso a young calf from Pal's back, but Taffy shied away at the last moment. Andi missed every time.

"It's all right, Taffy," she said, soothing her friend. "Chad and I will teach you to be the best cow pony on the ranch. You just need to be patient and grow up a little."

Chad laughed. "Look who's talking."

Andi scowled. She tried to be patient, but it was very hard when she was the youngest in the family. Everybody else could do so many more things than Andi. Even Melinda, and she was only five years older.

She bit back a sassy reply before it sneaked out. Chad was just teasing her, like always.

"Come on," Chad said. "I want to show you something."

Andi thought she knew every acre on the ranch. She was mistaken. Chad led her up into the hills, to a part of the ranch Andi had never explored. A bubbling creek cut through the pasture. Oak trees dotted the hills. In the distance, snowy mountains stood out against the blue sky.

Andi gasped. "It's beautiful!"

"It is, isn't it?" Chad smiled. "You should see it in early spring, when the wildflowers are blooming."

He showed Andi his name carved into one of the tree trunks. "I found this spot when I was a boy. Nobody ever comes up here. It's a good place to get off by yourself. I thought you might like it too."

"I do." Andi looked around. "But how will I find it again?"

"I'll show you when we head home," Chad promised. "It can be your special secret spot."

Andi squinted up at her brother. "You never showed this place to Mitch or Justin? Or to Melinda?"

Chad shook his head. "They might have found it on their own, but they never mentioned it. It's yours, Andi. It's also a great fishing spot."

He yanked Sky around. "Well, I've got a full day's work ahead of me, so we better get back."

Andi slumped. "So soon?"

"Yep. But cheer up. From what I can see, Taffy is completely saddle broke and calm as a summer day. Mother might want Melinda to ride along with you a few more times, but I see no reason why you can't ride Taffy on your own."

Andi cheered right up. "If you say so, then Mother will agree. I told you, Chad. Taffy's perfect in every way."

Andi nudged her filly to keep up with Sky. She paid careful attention to the landmarks Chad pointed out. She wanted to find her way back to her new special spot.

As they rode home together, Andi was thinking hard. Now that Chad agreed Taffy was a calm, safe horse, Andi wanted to ask him a question. It was a question she had been turning over in her mind for several weeks.

An important question.

CHAPTER 4

No Means No

Andi cleared her throat. Then she gripped the reins and asked her important question. "When can I learn to stand up on Taffy, like Riley used to do on Midnight?"

Remembering her friend Riley always made Andi sad. She missed him so much! She liked her town friends, but she only saw them at school. Riley had lived right here on the ranch. He stayed three whole years while his sick mother was getting better in far-off San Francisco.

Then six months ago, Riley's father stopped by the ranch. He packed up Riley, thanked Mother, Chad, and Uncle Sid—the ranch foreman—for keeping his boy, and off they went. Andi cried for three days after that.

She shook her head to get rid of the gloomy memories and looked at Chad. Hadn't he heard her question? She asked it again, but louder this time. Then she quickly added, "You said Taffy's calm as a summer day."

How fun it would be to stand up on her palomino's back, loping through a grassy field with her arms spread out wide! "Riley told me it feels just like flying. I bet Taffy and I could learn that trick in no time."

Please say yes, she silently begged.

"No." Chad's mouth turned down in a frown. "It's too dangerous. Sid should never have let his nephew fool around with such a risky stunt. It's a wonder Riley wasn't seriously hurt."

"But, Chad!" Andi wailed. "You told me no when I was six years old. I'm older now. Older than Riley was when he did it. He said it's easy as pie. He never fell off. You *have* to let me learn that trick."

"I don't have to let you do any such thing." Chad's eyes flashed. "If you try that or any other reckless stunt, you won't be riding Taffy at all."

Chad's answer dumped a big bucket of icy water all over Andi's great idea. Her birthday joy washed away.

She had been so sure her brother would let her learn Riley's stand-up trick when she was old enough. She had waited and waited. For what? To be reminded that everybody thought she was still a baby?

"I'm *not* a baby," Andi huffed. "And you're not Father. I'm going to ask Mother about it."

Chad's frown changed to a crooked smile. "You go right ahead, missy." He pointed between two hills. "The house is that way."

Without even a thank-you for the ride, Andi kicked Taffy's sides. The young horse bounded away. Andi heard Chad laughing in the distance.

She pouted. *Not funny! Chad is mean and bossy.*

By the time Andi trotted Taffy into the yard, however, she felt sorry for losing her temper. In her anger, she'd forgotten about her new saddle. She'd forgotten that Chad showed her the special spot. She'd even forgotten he told her she could ride Taffy out on the range by herself.

Andi sighed. Chad had an apology coming.

She would not ask Mother about the trick riding. Deep down, Andi already knew the answer. Mother let Chad make all the ranch decisions. He was the ranch boss.

Chad always gave Andi her outside chores. Chad picked the best times to help her train Taffy. Chad decided which horses Andi would ride, or if she could tag along with the crew during branding season.

Learning to trick ride on the Circle C was a ranch decision. If Chad said no, then Mother would go along with it. Didn't Andi expect Mother to go along with Chad's decision to let Andi ride Taffy alone?

"No wonder Chad laughed," Andi muttered. She led Taffy into the barn and took off her bridle. "He knew all along what Mother would say."

Taffy shook her creamy mane and rubbed her nose against the railing.

Andi carefully hung her new bridle and reins from a nearby nail.

The saddle was a different story. She shoved Coco's old saddle aside to make room for the new one. But it was much heavier than Andi thought. When she loosened the cinch and yanked, the leather seat came tumbling down. So did the saddle blanket.

Ooof!

Andi sat down hard, with the saddle and blanket on top of her. Dazed, she wondered how she would ever saddle Taffy by herself. She caught sight of Coco's saddle from the corner of her eye. It seemed to be laughing at her.

Andi wiggled out from under the heavy piece of tack and stood up. Frowning, she brushed herself off. She looked at her saddle on the barn floor. Then she looked at the railing.

It was a long way up, but she couldn't leave her beautiful new saddle lying on the ground.

She bent over, gripped the saddle horn with both hands, and yanked. It rose a foot. Step by slow step, Andi hauled her saddle toward the railing. Her star-studded stirrups dragged along the barn floor.

Andi groaned. "Oh no." She'd had her saddle for less than a day, and already it was a dusty mess.

Just then, Andi heard footsteps. Thank goodness! A ranch hand's help was just what she needed. She looked up.

"Having a little trouble?" With one hand, Chad took hold of the horn and tossed the saddle over the railing. It landed with a heavy *thunk*.

He brushed the dust from his hands. "You took off in an awful hurry. Glad to see you found your way home."

"I . . ." Andi stared at her boot tops. "I'm sorry I lost my temper."

Chad ruffled her hair, which meant he forgave her and wasn't mad. "After lunch, ask Sid to saddle Taffy," he said. "See if you can find your own way back to that special spot."

Andi's head snapped up. She grinned at her brother. "All right!"

He winked. "And next time you go riding, don't forget your hat."

⊰ CHAPTER 5 ⊱

Special Spot

*P*lop!

Andi's fishing line sank beneath the clear, still water. After riding up to her special spot, it had taken only a few minutes to find this quiet pool. The creek had long ago carved out part of the bank under an old oak tree, leaving a perfect fishing hole.

Several yards away, the rest of the creek splashed by. The water ran so fast in the springtime that it could carry Andi's fishing gear downstream if she wasn't careful.

Not good! Mitch might not want to whittle Andi a new pole. Nor would he want to give her another hook and sinker.

Andi gripped her pole tighter and looked down. The trout seemed to like this peaceful pool. Andi could see them swimming here and there. Trouble was, they weren't swimming anywhere near her hook.

She frowned. "I dug up these worms just for you. Don't you like them?"

Apparently not. Maybe the trout found them too scrawny to eat. Or maybe fish weren't hungry in the middle of the day.

Andi yanked her pole out of the water and leaned it against the tree trunk. It was a giant oak, with gnarled bark and low, spreading branches just right for climbing.

"All right then," Andi told the fish. "If you aren't biting, I'll climb this tree and wait until you're hungry."

She peeked at Taffy. Her filly sure was hungry. She bit the grass in quick, chomping mouthfuls. Then she walked a few steps and ate some more.

"Don't wander off," Andi told her horse.

Hand over hand, Andi climbed halfway up the tree. She settled herself on a thick branch. Then she leaned against the trunk and let her legs dangle. Peering between the leaves, she watched the creek tumble and splash out from the hills. It flowed down toward the faraway valley.

Andi let out a happy sigh. "This is the prettiest spot on the whole ranch."

It was the quietest spot too. Except for the rippling creek, Andi heard nothing. No rattling wagons. No galloping hoofbeats or bellowing cattle. No bossy brother telling her she couldn't—

Oops. Sorry, God. I forgot.

Chad could be really nice. He helped her train Taffy. He showed her this perfect spot. She had apologized for losing her temper, but that didn't mean she was happy about his decision. Why wouldn't he let her try one teensy-weensy riding trick?

"I might ask him again sometime." Maybe Chad would change his mind when he saw how careful she was with—

"Hey!"

Andi jerked from her daydreaming. It wasn't a ranch hand's voice. It wasn't Chad. Who could it be? Chad said nobody ever came up here. *Nobody.*

He was wrong.

Andi sat perfectly still and hoped the bushy oak leaves hid her. She didn't want a stranger invading her special spot. Especially not today, when she had only just claimed it. "Go away," she whispered.

"Anybody here? Whose horse is this?"

It sounded like a girl's voice, but it wasn't Melinda. Melinda already knew Taffy was Andi's horse. She would also know Andi was up in the tree. Melinda was an expert tree climber. She would probably climb up and join her.

Even though she told Andi every other day it wasn't ladylike to climb trees.

Andi spread the leaves apart. A barefoot girl wearing faded overalls sat on a brown horse. While Andi watched, the girl slid from the horse's back and walked up to Taffy. She rubbed the filly's nose then took hold of the reins.

"Hey!" the girl hollered. "I said, *whose horse is this?*" She looked around. Then she tugged on the reins. "I guess it's finders keepers, losers weepers."

Andi sucked in her breath. *Oh no it's not!* If this strange girl thought she was going to keep Taffy, she had another think coming.

Andi scrambled down the tree. When she reached the lowest branch, she swung from it and dropped to the ground. "*Hey* yourself! What are you doing? That's my horse."

The girl laughed. "I knew I could get you to show yourself." She dropped the reins. "Mighty pretty horse. I wouldn't really take her." She turned a full circle. "This your spread?"

Andi nodded. "Where did you come from?"

"Thataway." The girl pointed up the creek. "We got a place just on the other side of those hills. I been followin' this creek for quite a spell. Woulda kept goin' if I hadn't seen the horse."

"Why are you following our creek?"

She shrugged. "To see where it goes." She flipped a dirty-blond braid behind her shoulder. "What's your name?"

"Andi Carter. What's yours?"

"Sadie Hollister."

Andi's eyes widened in alarm. This girl had the same last name as the rude, black-bearded stranger at breakfast. She backed up a step. Maybe it was time to go home.

"What's the matter?" Sadie asked. "I don't bite."

"N-nothing." Andi swallowed. "It's just that a man barged into our house this morning and yelled at my brothers. His name was Hollister too."

"Betcha it was Pa," Sadie said. "He's a yeller. And he's awful mad at you Carters these days." She laughed. "But I'm not. I don't care about creeks changing course or spring floods washing away boundaries."

Andi made a face. "I don't care either."

"Mostly I like to follow creeks," Sadie said. "Never know what you might find. I followed that other creek's new course clear down to the valley. I like to fish too. Caught me a stringer full the other day. Ma was real happy to fry 'em up."

A whole stringer of fish?

Andi slumped on the inside. She couldn't catch even one fish today. But this girl—who appeared to be no older than Andi—caught stringers full. She rode all over other people's ranches. She even rode clear down to the valley all by herself.

Lucky!

"Hey, that's sure a beauty!" Sadie ran over and picked up Andi's fishing pole. "Looks almost store-bought." Before Andi could tell her Mitch made it, Sadie crossed to the creek. "Nice spot. Where's your stringer?"

Andi picked up her empty braided string. "Right here." She held out a tin can half full of dirt. "Here's my bait."

Sadie dumped the dirt into her hand. When she saw the worms, she piled the whole mess back inside the can. "You can't catch nothin' with those teensy things. Fat earthworms or doughballs work best."

Andi shook her head. "I tried doughballs once. They don't work."

"My doughballs work," Sadie said. "It's a secret recipe. I catch trout long as your arm with 'em."

"Really? Would you give me the recipe?"

Sadie frowned and chewed the end of her braid. "I might tell a friend my secret recipe," she said at last. She brushed her hair aside. "I sometimes get tired of seeing only kinfolk."

Andi knew how Sadie felt. Ever since Riley had left the ranch, she missed having a playmate her own age nearby.

"You want to be friends?" Sadie asked.

Easy question. "Sure."

Sadie's dirty face broke into a smile. "Al-righty!" She eyed Taffy. "I got a jim-dandy idea, Andi. How

45

about a trade? I'll bring fresh doughballs next Saturday. You can try 'em out and see how good they work."

Visions of arm-length trout swam in Andi's head. Wouldn't Mitch be surprised! He was the best fisherman in the family. But not for long. "What's the trade?"

Sadie pointed at Taffy. "Doughballs in exchange for a ride on your fancy saddle."

Andi nodded. "It's a deal."

"Yippee!" Sadie sprang onto Taffy's back. Before Andi could blink, her new friend urged Taffy into a gentle lope.

Then, to Andi's everlasting surprise, Sadie stood up.

CHAPTER 6

New Friend

All week long Andi daydreamed about the fish she would catch on Saturday. When she closed her eyes, she saw trout snapping up doughballs as fast as she dropped her hook into the water.

Andi tried not to see Sadie in her thoughts. Sadie on Taffy. Sadie doing Riley's trick. Andi squeezed her eyes shut even tighter. *Can everybody in California trick ride but me?*

Daydreaming about catching trout made studying arithmetic hard. Thinking about Sadie's stand-up trick made paying attention during Friday's spelling bee impossible.

"Andrea Carter!"

Miss Hall's sharp voice jerked Andi from her thoughts. She found herself back at the blackboard, standing with twenty-four other pupils. Everybody looked at her. Two boys snickered.

Andi's cheeks grew warm. "Ma'am?"

"Enough woolgathering," the teacher scolded. "It's your turn. Spell *trowel*, please."

"T-trowel," Andi stammered. Her head felt full of Taffy and trout. "T-R-O-U-T," she spelled without thinking.

The class roared with laughter.

Andi returned to her seat in disgrace. She buried her head in her arms and wished she didn't have to go to school. Sadie didn't go to school. At least, Andi had never seen her here.

Sadie had told Andi she lived way up in the hills. Mother said most hill people were poor and worked hard just to earn a living. Maybe Sadie was too poor to go to school. Or maybe she lived too far away.

⊰ ⊱

"I wish I lived too far away to go to school," Andi said at breakfast Saturday morning.

"If wishes were horses . . ." Mitch began.

". . . beggars would ride," Melinda finished with a giggle.

Andi rolled her eyes. Mitch and Melinda chanted that nursery rhyme every time Andi wished for something. She knew wishing didn't make anything happen.

She also knew that not going to school was never going to happen—at least not for a long, long time.

Andi worked at her Saturday chores extra fast, but it was noon before she finally stepped off the back porch. She shaded her eyes. As usual, she would have to ask somebody to saddle Taffy.

A friendly whinny made Andi smile in surprise. Taffy stood tied to the railing, saddled and ready to go. Andi's hat hung over the saddle horn.

Mitch was leaning Andi's fishing pole against the barn. "Here you go, Sis," he called.

"Thanks, Mitch." Andi jammed her hat down on her head and climbed up on Taffy. "I'm going to bring you the biggest fish, just for being so nice."

Mitch chuckled and handed up her fishing gear. "Sure you are. Where's your bait?"

"You'll see."

Andi waved good-bye. Then she galloped Taffy all the way to her special spot. She hadn't meant to be so late. What if Sadie had given up and gone home?

She hadn't.

When Andi pulled Taffy to a stop, Sadie jumped up from her place by the pool. "Took you long enough." She lifted a stringer of fish from the water. "Looky here."

Andi dismounted. "Oh my!" Three big, wriggling trout hung on the line. "Are there any fish left?" Worry crept into her voice.

Sadie dropped the stringer back into the water. "Plenty." She waved Andi over. Opening a tin bucket, she dug around inside.

"This here is a doughball." She plopped a yellowish glob of pastry in Andi's hand. "A little cornmeal, some flour, soft cheese from our sheep, and a heap of garlic."

Andi wrinkled her nose at the smell. *Disgusting!*

Sadie lowered her voice. "The secret is a pinch of white sugar. When I can sneak it. Then boil 'em like dumplings and lay 'em out to dry." She shoved Andi toward the water. "Try it."

Andi crammed the stinky ball onto her hook. Then she dropped her line into the sparkling water and waited.

She didn't wait long. The trout bit so fast that Andi almost lost her pole. She held on with all her might. "Help!"

Sadie grabbed the fishing pole. They both yanked.

The trout flew out of the water. It flopped around on the creek bank for a minute then lay still, gasping.

"It's gotta be three pounds at least," Sadie said.

"Those doughballs work," Andi whispered, astonished. She threw her arms around Sadie and hugged her tight. "They really work!"

"I told you so."

Andi caught ten more fish in less than an hour. Then Sadie gave Andi her fish too. "We ate trout last night and the night before. Ma's sick of fish."

"I can't carry all these home by myself," Andi said. "Plus my fishing gear."

Sadie grinned. "I'll help you."

It took both girls to lift Andi's heavy stringer and tie it around the saddle horn. The wet, scaly fish dripped down Andi's new saddle.

Sadie tied her stringer to Andi's saddle horn too. Trout now dripped down both sides.

"I hope I can scrub my saddle clean of all the fish stink," Andi said.

Sadie laughed and mounted her horse. She held their poles and the bait can in one hand. "Let's get going before those fish rot in the heat."

Mitch was not there when Andi and Sadie trotted into the yard. Neither was Chad. Or Mother. Or Justin or Melinda.

Only Luisa *oohed* and *aahed* over Andi's splendid catch. "I will take those fish," she called from the back porch. "Such a fish fry we will have tonight!"

Andi was happy to be rid of them. Catching fish was fun. Cleaning fish was not. A dead fish was slimy and *very* slippery. But trout sure tasted good the way Luisa fixed them.

Sadie was a big help in the barn. With both of them carrying it, Andi's saddle made it to the railing without falling to the ground even once. A good thing too. Dirt stuck to leftover, sticky fish even after they were gone.

Something else stuck to fish stink too. Flies. Dozens of them. They buzzed around the girls' heads. Andi swiped at the flies and worked faster. Sadie didn't seem to notice them.

But she did notice the cats. Five had followed the fish smell and were rubbing their heads against Andi's legs. A small black cat with white splotches meowed at Sadie and pushed against her bare ankle.

She grinned. "You got some real nice cats, Andi."

Andi wiped her sticky hands down the sides of her overalls and picked up the cat. It immediately started licking her fingers. "This is Licorice, on account of he's black and likes to eat licorice."

Sadie's jaw dropped. "You name your barn cats?"

"Yep." Andi pointed to the others. "That's Mouser, Ticktock, Rice, and Buttons. Bella has a litter up in the loft."

"Kittens!" Sadie exclaimed softly. Her blue eyes gleamed. "Can we play with them?"

"Sure. But why would you want to? Don't you have cats?"

"Half-wild ones." Sadie held up her arm. A thin red scar ran from her wrist to her elbow. "If you get too close, they scratch you to ribbons." She shook her head. "And they sure don't got no names."

After the girls brushed and groomed Taffy, Andi led her new friend up the ladder and into the loft.

Tied bundles of alfalfa and loose hay covered the floor. In a back corner, Andi found Bella with four young kittens. The mama cat purred, clearly happy to see Andi.

The kittens pounced and climbed all over the girls. They attacked Sadie's bare toes and pieces of wiggling straw. Andi and Sadie fell laughing into the hay.

Bella left her babies in good hands and went off to hunt. She returned a few minutes later with a plump mouse in her mouth. Playtime was over.

"I better go," Sadie said. "Ma will skin me alive if I stay away too long."

Licorice climbed into the hayloft just then and rubbed against Andi and Sadie, purring loudly. Ticktock and Mouser followed him.

Sadie sighed. "Wish I had me a cat." She grinned. "A nice one, I mean."

Andi looked at Sadie in surprise. "You want another cat?" She waved her arm around the loft. "Pick any one you want. Mother says our barn is overflowing with cats."

"You mean it?" She grabbed Licorice. "I'll take this one."

Andi nodded. "I'll find a gunnysack so you can take him home."

The girls scooted across the loft floor.

Just then, two men and their horses blocked the

sunlight. They didn't come inside the barn, but stood in the doorway and talked.

Andi swung her leg over the ladder.

"Wait!" Sadie gripped Andi's shoulder. "Who are those men?"

⊰ CHAPTER 7 ⊱

Surprises

Andi paused, one leg dangling over the top rung. "What men?" She glanced at the doorway. "Oh. It's just my brother and our ranch foreman." She climbed down the ladder. "Come on."

Andi skipped across the barn then poked around in a corner for a gunnysack.

Sadie darted to her side, clutching Licorice. She stared at the men. Her eyes were round and scared.

"What's the matter?" Andi asked. She picked up a burlap sack and shook off the dust. She sneezed.

Sadie pointed to Chad. "He came out to our place and yelled at Ma and us kids."

"Like your father did at my house?"

Sadie's face turned red. "Oh. You're right."

"Don't mind Chad. He's just . . ." Andi thought

of the word he had used at breakfast last Saturday. "He's just all *bluster*."

Sadie nodded and quietly stroked Licorice. In the silence, it was easy to hear what Chad was saying.

"Listen, Sid. I want a good, strong fence put up between Hollister's place and ours before next week. I don't care if it takes every man we've got. Do it."

Sid shrugged. "Sure thing, boss. But that's a mighty long stretch of fence you've got in mind."

"The longer the better," Chad said. "Strong fences make good neighbors." He clapped Sid on the shoulder and sent him on his way. Then he led Sky into the barn.

"Howdy, Chad," Andi called. She held up the gunnysack. "I'm giving my friend Sadie a cat."

"Only one?" Chad winked at Sadie. "Are you sure you don't want two or three more?"

Andi giggled, but Sadie shook her head. "No. One's good. At least for now." She brushed by Chad and left the barn.

Andi hurried after her.

It took a bit of work, but Licorice finally gave in to being stuffed inside the scratchy burlap sack. Andi got a piece of raw fish from Luisa and threw it in the sack. The cat's yowling turned into low growls.

Sadie scrambled up on her horse. She picked up the reins and reached for the sack. "He's a jim-dandy

cat," she told Andi. "It's mighty nice of you to give him to me."

"Like Chad said, you can have more if you want." Andi wrinkled her forehead. "Except maybe not Bella. She's my special cat."

Licorice's growls grew deeper. Pretty soon he'd start yowling again.

"I better go," Sadie said. "Wait till the little kids see my prize!" She turned her horse toward the hills. Just before she galloped off, she leaned close to Andi. "You come out to my place next Saturday. I got a surprise for you." She patted the gunnysack. "In trade for this here cat you gave me."

"More doughballs?"

Sadie laughed. "No. Somethin' better. Bye!"

⚞ ⚟

The last week of school dragged by slower than a turtle race.

At recess Andi told Cory about her new friend. She left out the part about the secret doughball recipe. For sure Cory would want to know more. He was the second-best fisherman Andi knew, after Mitch.

Andi didn't think she should share a secret recipe without permission.

To Andi's surprise, Cory already knew about Sadie.

He shook his blond head. "I hear the Hollisters are a wild, mean bunch. Don't mess with them."

Andi stood up for her friend. "Sadie's nice. I like her. We're going fishing on Saturday. Want to come?"

"Yeah, but I can't." Cory made a face. "Pa needs my help mucking out the livery stable."

Andi made a face too. She hated cleaning stalls worse than anything.

⚞ ⚟

On Saturday, Andi took care of Taffy's stall in a hurry. She wanted to play with Sadie the rest of the day. She rubbed her new saddle until every bit of dirt disappeared. Then she polished the conchos until they sparkled.

When she finished her chores, Mitch saddled Taffy. Andi gave him a hug and promised him the biggest trout from today's catch.

This time Mitch believed her.

But at the creek, Sadie didn't give Andi time to catch even one fish. She was too excited about taking Andi home with her.

The two girls rode for what seemed to Andi like hours and hours. The sun told the truth though. It had barely moved across the sky when Sadie and Andi splashed their horses across Spring Creek's new course. A few minutes later, they pulled to a stop next to the Circle C ranch's old boundary.

Andi shaded her eyes. The creek bed was wide and dry. Brand-new wooden fence posts stuck up all along the center of the creek. Four shiny strands of barbed wire ran both ways as far as Andi could see.

"This fence goes on forever," she said.

Sadie shook her head. "It won't be there for long. Pa will see to that. He's madder than a hornet."

Andi gulped. If Mr. Hollister tore down the fence, Chad would be madder than a whole *nest* of hornets.

Sadie jabbed her heels into her horse's sides. "Giddup, Jep. Come on, Andi."

The girls had to ride a long way to go around the fence, but at last they topped a small hill. Sadie pointed. "There's my place." They started downhill.

Nothing in all of Andi's nine years had prepared her for what she saw when she pulled Taffy to a stop in the yard. The house was little more than a shack. A rickety porch poked out from the front. It was missing a step. A thin curl of smoke rose from a crumbling stone chimney.

Sadie sniffed the air and rubbed her belly. "Just in time. Tie up your horse and come on in."

Andi followed a barefoot Sadie around broken tools, a sorry-looking woodpile, and heaps of rubbish. When she stepped through the doorway, Andi froze.

The black-bearded stranger from breakfast two weeks ago sat at the head of the table. He glared at her. Ten other pairs of eyes stared at Andi from filthy faces.

One face was creased with more wrinkles than a walnut. "Who are you?" the old woman demanded in a shrill voice.

Sadie pushed a small girl aside and sat down. "This here's my friend Andi. She's hungry."

No, I'm not. Andi stared at a tin plate heaped with some kind of stew mashed together in one brownish lump.

Sadie yanked Andi down beside her. "Don't mind Granny."

"I know who she is," Mr. Hollister said gruffly. "She's the Carter girl."

"Humph!" The old woman's scowl deepened.

Sadie's mother smiled. "Go on and have a bite, child, before it gets cold."

With those words, the whole family ignored Andi and tore into their meal.

Andi knew it would be rude not to eat, so she took a tiny bite. Then she took a bigger spoonful. The yucky-looking stew tasted delicious, and she said so.

Mrs. Hollister beamed. "It's mutton."

Andi wrinkled her forehead. "What's mutton?"

A boy who looked a little older than Sadie laughed. "Sheep meat, you dum—"

"Enough, Zeke," Mr. Hollister cut in. "Her family don't raise sheep. They raise . . . beef."

Granny snorted.

Andi's cheeks grew warm. Mr. Hollister made it sound like they grew poison on the Circle C ranch. She ducked her head.

Mrs. Hollister rapped the table with her spoon. "That's no way to treat a guest. Mind your manners, y'hear? You too, Granny. Sadie, you and Andi take the little kids outside. Pa's in a sour mood. Best leave him be."

Andi couldn't get away fast enough. Sadie's mother was nice, but Mr. Hollister's growly voice made shivers run up Andi's neck. And Granny? Andi wanted nothing to do with her.

"Want to see our sheep?" Sadie asked.

Andi brightened. "Yes!" She liked sheep. She remembered digging her fingers into thick, soft wool when she went to the fair.

Three raggedy children trailed behind Andi and Sadie on their way to the pasture. It was a large area, but the sheep had chewed the grass right down to the dirt and rocks. *Baa, baa!* They sounded hungry.

No wonder Mr. Hollister wanted fresh grazing land.

Sadie reached into a nearly empty sack and passed out handfuls of dried corn. When she and Andi climbed into the pasture, the sheep crowded around to get their share. They butted and bleated until Andi was laughing so hard she could barely keep her balance.

Then Sadie showed Andi a dirty-white lamb. It was much smaller than the plump lambs skipping next to their mothers. It baaed a lot. Sadie dragged it under the fence and out of the field. Andi climbed over the wobbly railings and joined her.

"It's a bum lamb," Sadie said. "His mama won't have nothin' to do with him." She picked up the lamb and shoved it into Andi's arms. "This here's my surprise. You gave me a cat. I'm givin' you this lamb."

CHAPTER 8

Show-Offs

Andi gasped. "For me?"

Under her hands, Andi could feel the lamb's ribs and its thumping heart. Her own heart skipped a beat. She'd had a lamb once, for about ten minutes at the state fair. Andi had won the lamb, but Chad wouldn't let her keep it. And Mother backed him up.

But now? A lamb of her own!

A moment later, a gloomy thought spoiled Andi's delight. *I can't keep this lamb either.*

Her brothers were cattlemen. They didn't like sheep. None of the Circle C cowhands liked sheep. They wouldn't let a sheep step one hoof onto the ranch. What's more, Chad didn't want to give up his good grazing land to Mr. Hollister's flock of smelly, four-footed pests.

Wasn't that what the whole boundary argument was about?

Andi couldn't keep the lamb, but how would she tell Sadie? Her friend looked so pleased with her surprise. "Your father might not like me taking it," Andi said.

Sadie shrugged. "Pa don't care nothin' for this lamb. I'm the only one that takes time now and then to feed it."

Andi swallowed. "I can't take it." She forced her words out. "My brother—"

"You . . ." Sadie's face fell. "You don't want it?"

Andi's heart squeezed at Sadie's crushed expression. *I hurt her feelings.* She snuggled the lamb closer. "I *do* want it," she said quickly. "Thank you." *I'll think of some way to keep it.*

Sadie's eyes sparkled, and she grinned. "Al-righty!"

Andi glanced up. The sun was halfway to the horizon. "I hope I can find my way home."

Sadie shook out the grain sack. Corn flew everywhere. "We can stuff the lamb in here. I'll get his bottle and go with you as far as your fishing spot. You know the way home from there."

Andi followed Sadie back to the yard. She was so busy thinking how she would keep the lamb that she didn't notice the empty hitching post.

"Zeke! Tom! You get back here right now!"

Sadie's face was red with fury. "I'm gonna put a

snake in your bed if you don't come back," she hollered. "Maybe even a rattlesnake!"

It took Andi two seconds to learn the reason why.

Taffy was no longer tied up. Instead, Sadie's brother Zeke stood on the filly's back with his arms outstretched. One hand gripped Taffy's reins. He turned her in a big circle and kept riding.

An older boy stood on Sadie's horse. The boys did the stand-up trick like they'd done it all their lives. They did it better than Riley ever did.

Andi's mouth dropped open in astonishment. She ignored the lamb's squirming.

"Show-offs!" Sadie yelled. She turned to Andi. "They won't hurt your horse. They're just showin' off."

More than anything Andi wanted to learn that trick. It looked so easy. Even Sadie could do it. "How did they learn it?" she asked.

"We been doin' it since we was tiny." Sadie pointed to a little boy playing in the dirt. "Even Jonah can do it. Pa learned when he was a boy working in the circus. He used to sneak into the big circus tent and practice."

Andi looked at Jonah. He was half Andi's size. "Do you ever fall off?"

Sadie laughed. "All the time."

Just then Taffy took a sharp turn. Zeke squealed, lost his footing, and slid off the saddle. He hit the

ground and lay still. The next moment he leaped up and caught Taffy's reins before she could run away.

Sadie dropped the empty grain sack and ran after him. "You showed off long enough." She yanked the reins out of his hands. "Leave her horse be." Without waiting for his say-so, she brought Taffy back to Andi.

Taffy did not look any worse for the trick riding. She wasn't sweaty. Her ears were pricked forward, like she'd enjoyed it. Her eyes looked bright but peaceful. She shook her mane and whickered.

"Did you like that, girl?" Andi asked.

"Your horse is a natural." Sadie rubbed Taffy's nose. "Smart and calm. I could teach you the trick."

Tingles raced up and down Andi's arms. Sadie could teach her, and nobody would ever know. She eagerly squeezed her lamb.

No, you can't.

The quiet words whispered in Andi's head. Her thrill crashed to her toes. *No means no,* she thought. She sighed and shook her head. "I can't. Not today."

Andi didn't tell Sadie that she could *never* learn it. Maybe Chad would change his mind if he knew what good trick riders the Hollister kids were. After all, they'd learned it from a real circus person.

It was getting too late to talk anymore about trick riding. If Andi didn't return home soon, Mother would worry. She'd send somebody up to the special spot to bring Andi home. If Andi wasn't there, Mother would worry even more, and she might not let Andi visit Sadie again.

Sadie held the large sack open, but Andi couldn't get the lamb into it. Zeke finally stuffed most of the lamb inside. Sadie tossed in the bottle. Then Zeke tied the sack around the lamb's neck so it could stick its head out to breathe.

Baa, baa! The lamb did not like being tied up in a sack.

Zeke lifted the heavy sack and tied it around Andi's saddle horn. He didn't act mean or impatient about helping her. Maybe he was making up for riding Taffy.

Andi didn't ask. The sinking sun prodded her to hurry.

All the way back to Andi's special spot the lamb bleated. And wriggled. And bumped against Taffy's left side. Every time the lamb's hoof kicked through the sack, Taffy put her ears back and whinnied. Once, she even gave a little hop.

But Andi was an excellent rider. She kept Taffy under control, even when her filly broke into a gallop. "Easy, girl," Andi said. "I know you want to get away from that bumping bag. It won't be long."

Finally, the lamb no longer bleated. By the time they made it back to Andi's special spot, it had fallen asleep and lay like a limp rag. Taffy settled right down.

Sadie laughed. "I hope you make it home in one piece." She handed Andi her fishing pole. "You sure got your hands full." She waved good-bye and dug her heels into Jep. "See you next Saturday!"

Andi turned toward home and prodded her filly into a gallop. "We have to get Snowball home quick," she told Taffy. "If he wakes up, he'll baa his head off."

Taffy snorted and galloped faster.

Andi let her hat fly off her head and hang down her back. The string dug into her neck, but she ignored it. "I'll get some milk from Cook. He won't ask any questions."

As soon as Andi rode into the yard, she jumped off Taffy and led her into the barn. Nobody was around. *So far, so good.* She untied the rope from her saddle horn. Zeke had made the knot easy to pull loose.

Andi carried Snowball into Taffy's stall and let him go. The lamb staggered a bit before falling on the straw.

Andi dug the bottle out of the sack. "I'll be right back," she promised.

The Mexican ranch cook acted gruff, like always. He scolded Andi for bothering him, but he gave her a bucket of fresh milk without asking why.

A few minutes later, Snowball's belly was full. He lay down in a corner and went to sleep.

Andi tiptoed outside. She found a ranch hand

who was happy to unsaddle Taffy. Afterward, Andi led her filly into the stall and brushed her.

"Snowball will have to hide in your stall until I figure out a way to keep him," Andi told her filly. "After all, I can't hurt Sadie's feelings, can I?"

Taffy chomped on her alfalfa and snorted.

Andi smiled. "I knew you would agree." She looked fondly at the sleeping lamb. As long as Snowball's belly stayed full, he would keep quiet.

At least Andi hoped he would.

CHAPTER 9

Trouble

Keeping Snowball quiet and hidden was hard work. The next morning, before anybody else got up, Andi jumped out of bed. She filled Snowball's bottle and fed him. That way he stayed quiet when her brothers came out to the barn for their horses.

Andi did her chores without being reminded. She went in and out of the barn all day, letting her lamb gulp down milk whenever he wanted.

She rubbed his fuzzy head. "You're going to be the fattest lamb in three counties."

Snowball's belly stuck out round and fat from all that milk. It also made him frisky. He butted Taffy and leaped high into the air. He chased Andi around Taffy's stall. Then he lay down for a nap.

Later that day, Andi and Snowball romped outside

in the fenced area behind Taffy's stall. No ranch hands hung around the yard during busy afternoons. The lamb followed Andi just like Mary's little lamb from the nursery rhyme. It was easy to sneak him in and out of the stall.

It was *not* easy to think of a good way to tell Mother about Snowball. Andi kept putting it off. She knew it was only a matter of time before somebody discovered her new pet. But the right time never came up.

Three days later, it was too late to tell Mother. Or anybody else.

"Andi!" Chad yelled.

Andi peeked out between the branches of the tree she'd just climbed. She held a cookie in one hand. A rope hung over her other arm. She was just about to make a rope swing.

Below her, Chad held a squirming, kicking lamb at arm's length. *"Andi!"* he yelled again. "Where are you?"

Andi dropped her rope. She stuffed the cookie in her mouth and scrambled out of the tree. "Put down my lamb!" she shouted around a mouthful of crumbs.

Baa, baa! Snowball thrashed and bleated. He did not like dangling in midair.

"So, this lamb belongs to you," Chad said. "I thought so. Sid found it in the barn." He sighed. "Where in the world did you get it?"

Andi pulled Snowball into her arms. He instantly stopped bleating. "From Sadie. She traded me for the cat."

"*Ohhh . . .*" Chad let out a long, slow breath, like he suddenly put two and two together. "Sadie *Hollister*? She's your friend?"

Andi nodded and put Snowball down. He stayed close to her side. "Sadie's lots of fun."

"I'm sure she is." Chad paused. "Listen, Andi. I hate to tell you this, but the lamb has to go back to the Hollisters."

"But—"

"No buts. If this was a sheep ranch, I would have let you keep the last one. Now, go get Taffy." When she hesitated, Chad nudged her. "Hurry up. I haven't got all day."

Andi kicked the dirt but did what her brother said. It was no use running to Mother. Andi knew this was another ranch decision Chad got to make. *What will Sadie think?*

She bridled Taffy then held Snowball while Chad saddled her filly.

All the way to Sadie's, Andi pouted. She glanced at Snowball. He lay across the front of Chad's saddle. Chad held the lamb down with one hand. His other hand gripped the reins.

"It's not the end of the world," Chad said in a soft voice. "When you're older you'll understand. We raise cattle and horses. Sheep are . . ." He cleared his throat. "Well, we don't raise sheep."

"Not even one?" Andi asked. "It will hurt Sadie's feelings if I give Snowball back."

Chad sighed. "I'm sorry, Andi, but that's the way it has to be—"

He broke off and jerked Sky to a halt. "Oh no! This is the last straw." He jabbed Sky in the sides and galloped away, with Snowball bleating at the top of his lungs.

Andi easily kept up. Just ahead lay the dried-up streambed and the new fence.

Or what was left of it.

Several fence posts had been chopped into chunks of firewood. Pieces of shiny barbed wire lay on the ground. A large flock of sheep grazed on the Circle C side of the old creek bed.

Without a word, Chad dumped the lamb with the rest of the sheep. Then he pushed Sky to a full gallop and headed straight for the Hollisters.

Andi didn't know what to do. Snowball was playing with the other lambs. Chad had left her and galloped away. She thought for a moment. Sadie needed to know about her lamb's homecoming.

"Hey, wait for me!" she shouted at Chad. Andi dug her heels into Taffy and took off after her brother.

As soon as Andi arrived at the Hollister place she wished she'd stayed with the sheep. Chad and

Mr. Hollister stood arguing in the middle of the cluttered yard. The Hollister family huddled on the porch, watching.

Andi slid off Taffy and ran to Sadie's side.

"You couldn't wait two weeks, could you?" Chad was saying. For once, he was not yelling. But he sounded angry, nonetheless. "Justin asked you to wait for the courts to settle this. But no! Instead, you tore down our fence. Your sheep are grazing on our land—"

"*My* land!" Mr. Hollister bellowed. "God moved that boundary, and no fancy court can say anything different."

Chad put his fists on his hips. "We'll see about that. When the judge makes his ruling, then and only then will I agree with you."

"Judge or no judge, I'll tear down any fence you put up, boy." Mr. Hollister raised his shotgun. "And from now on I'll shoot any Carter that steps foot on my land or comes near my place."

Andi shivered. Mr. Hollister did not sound full of bluster today. He sounded like he really meant it. *Please, God,* she prayed, *don't let Mr. Hollister shoot my brother.*

Sadie put her arms around Andi. "I'm scared," she whispered.

"S-so am I." Andi's voice shook. "All we wanted to do was bring back your lamb. Chad wouldn't let me keep it." She sniffed. "I want to go home."

"I can see why," Sadie said. "Pa's sure on a rant."

Mr. Hollister kept his weapon steady. "Now, get off my land. Don't come back." He paused. "Or else."

Chad eyed the shotgun and stepped back. "This isn't over."

Mr. Hollister waved his shotgun toward Sky. "Mount up and get goin'."

Andi untangled herself from Sadie's tight hold. "I better go. See you Saturday?"

Sadie nodded.

"Come on, Andi," Chad said. "Let's get out of here."

Chad didn't seem to be in any hurry to get home. He and Andi trotted their horses through the old creek boundary. They circled around the flock of sheep tearing at the rich spring grass.

Circle C grass.

Chad glanced over his shoulder.

Andi looked too. One of the older Hollister boys sat next to the creek bed. A shotgun rested across his knees.

Chad shook his head and prodded Sky. "I don't want you going near the Hollister place," he told Andi. "Do you hear me?"

Andi stared at Taffy's creamy mane. She heard him, all right. But that didn't mean she agreed. What did the grown-ups' problems have to do with her and Sadie?

"You stay away from all of them," Chad went on. "That whole Hollister bunch is crazy."

"Sadie's not. She doesn't have anything to do with—"

"You heard me," Chad cut in. "Vince Hollister might shoot you the next time he sees you. He knows you're a Carter."

Andi said nothing. Her throat was too tight to speak. But she was thinking a lot. *You are mean and—*

"I know you think I'm mean and bossy," Chad said. "But Mother will tell you the same thing. It's for your own good."

Andi didn't say no. She didn't say yes either. "I'm going to my special spot," she said.

Without waiting for Chad's say-so, Andi nudged Taffy and they galloped away.

⊰ CHAPTER 10 ⊱

The Accident

Mother told Andi the same thing Chad had told her. But Mother said it nicer. She pulled Andi close to her on Friday evening and explained that the Hollister place was not safe.

"At least not for now," she added.

"I won't go there, Mother," Andi promised. She took a deep breath. "Can't we pray for them? We can pray Mr. Hollister won't be so mean as to shoot anybody or . . ."

Andi's heart leaped at her next idea. Why hadn't she thought of it sooner? "We can pray that God sends a flood to put the creek back where it belongs."

Mother smiled. "That would be lovely, darling. But God might want the creek to stay where He put it this spring. It's better to pray that God will help us all get along, no matter who wins the boundary war." She looked straight at Chad. "Right, son?"

Chad gave Mother a crooked smile. "Right." Then he went back to beating Mitch at checkers—for the third time in a row.

The next day was Saturday. Andi piled the last of the doughballs Sadie had given her into her bait can. No matter what, Andi was not going to let any grown-up argument spoil her new fishing spot.

What if Sadie shows up?

Andi pushed her troubling thought aside. Mr. Hollister had no doubt told his daughter to stay away from the Carters. He would never let Sadie play with Andi again.

"I guess I won't see her," Andi told Taffy as they trotted along. "But if she does come to my special spot, I won't be rude. I won't tell a guest on the Circle C ranch to get lost."

Andi nudged Taffy from a bouncy trot into a smooth lope. Just ahead, she spied the giant oak tree hanging over her fishing spot. She smiled. Even without Sadie along, Andi would have a jim-dandy time catching trout.

When Andi pulled up under the tree, she gulped back her surprise. Sadie sat on the creek bank. Her legs dangled in the pool, along with her fishing line.

She looked up when Andi dropped from the saddle. "So, you came after all."

"Why wouldn't I come?" Andi asked. "This is my own special spot on the ranch."

Sadie narrowed her eyes. "Are you gonna kick me off your precious ranch?"

Her words lit a fire in Andi's belly. "Course not." She slammed her pole and bait can on the ground. Then she sat down hard. "But my brother says I have to stay away from you and your family."

"I know. Same here." Sadie yanked her pole from the water and threw it down. "I don't feel like fishin'." She looked ready to cry. "Why do grown-ups have to fight about the dumbest things? Your family owns *thousands* of acres."

Andi ducked her head at Sadie's angry outburst.

"Our sheep are hungry," Sadie said. "Our rangeland is worn out. Pa didn't know what he was gonna do this spring. Then the creek flooded and changed its course. That saved our sheep."

Her voice rose. "Why does your family care so much about a couple hundred acres way up in the hills?"

Andi didn't know why they cared. She didn't know anything about landrights, boundaries, and the law. But she did know what Chad had said at supper last night. It was a matter of principle. Of what was right and wrong. And when Chad thought he was right, nobody could change his mind.

Well, nobody except God.

Andi didn't tell Sadie any of this. Her friend looked upset enough already.

Andi was angry too, but not at Sadie. She wasn't mad about the creek changing course. She didn't care about sheep or cattle. She for sure didn't care about fences.

Right now Andi only cared about one thing. Just when she had found a playmate her own age, *whoosh!* Bossy Chad ripped her friend away.

The tiny flame in Andi's belly grew to a fiery blaze. "Chad ruins all my fun. Snowball was my best lamb ever. Well, my only lamb, but who's counting? I'm sorry I had to give him back." Hot tears swam in her eyes.

"That's all right." Sadie sighed. "Do you want Licorice back?" She didn't sound angry anymore. Only sad.

Andi shook her head. Her braids slapped her face. "I gave you Licorice. You didn't have to give me a lamb."

The more Andi talked, the more she felt like a runaway train engine. Waves of anger swept her along, blocking out any sensible thoughts. "Plus, do you know what else Chad told me?"

"No, what?" Sadie asked.

"I'm plenty old enough, but Chad won't let me learn Riley's stand-up trick."

"Who's Riley?"

"My best friend," Andi said. "He left the ranch

six months ago. Riley could do the best tricks ever. Just like you and your brothers. He said the stand-up trick is easy as pie."

Sadie shrugged. "It is."

"Chad said no. He won't even let me try. He won't teach—"

"Ha!" Sadie laughed. "He probably doesn't know how to do it." She gave Andi a sneaky look. "That's why he won't teach you."

Andi's thoughts came to a crashing halt. Was that the real reason Chad wouldn't teach her? He said it was dangerous, but did Chad only say that because he didn't know how to do the trick himself?

No fair!

She looked at Taffy. Her filly was grazing in the grassy field next to Sadie's horse, Jep. They looked like good friends, just like Andi and Sadie.

"I told you the other day," Sadie said. "Taffy's a natural. You saw me on her, and Zeke too. She won't give you no trouble. She's smart and calm."

"Calm as a summer day," Andi said under her breath. Her thoughts buzzed inside her head like a swarm of angry bees. *Just because Chad doesn't know the trick is no reason not to let me learn it.*

This new thought stuck in Andi's mind. She licked her lips and tried to swallow. Her throat felt drier than dust. She cleared it and said, "Teach me the trick."

Sadie bounded to her feet and grabbed Andi's hand. "Al-righty!"

A minute later Jep was tied up out of the way and Andi sat in Taffy's saddle. Her hands felt sweaty. She wiped them down the sides of her overalls. *Just one time*, she told herself. *Chad doesn't need to know.*

What about Mother? a quiet voice whispered back.

Andi's stomach turned over. Mother was a different story. What would she say when—

"Stand up." Sadie's instructions yanked Andi from her thoughts. "We'll go slow at first. Soon as you feel steady, I'll hand up the reins. Simple as that." She held Taffy's bridle.

Andi brought her feet up and kneeled on Taffy. She trembled from head to toe.

Why am I so shaky?

Hardly anything frightened Andi. She jumped aboard nearly every horse on the Circle C. She galloped them like the wind. She climbed trees to the tippy-top. She helped brand calves with a hot iron. She wasn't even afraid of the dark.

Something was very wrong.

Andi's heart pounded inside her chest so hard it made her gasp. Taffy's ears flicked back and forth. She shifted nervously. Andi gripped the saddle horn.

"Andi!" Sadie huffed her impatience. "Don't let your horse know you're scared."

"I'm not scared!" But the quivering in her arms and legs would not go away.

"Then stand up."

Andi slowly rose. Her legs felt wobbly. She planted her feet firmly on the saddle and spread her arms out to keep her balance.

Don't do it!

Right then Andi knew why she was so scared. She wasn't afraid of falling off Taffy. She was afraid of disobeying her mother.

I can't do this. But before she could jump down, Jep whinnied . . .

And everything happened at once.

Taffy whinnied back. She yanked her head out of Sadie's grip and headed straight for the tree where Jep was tied.

"Sit down!" Sadie yelled.

Too late.

Andi saw the thick branch just before she hit it.

Everything went black.

⊰ CHAPTER 11 ⊱

Painful Lesson

Andi woke up crying. She couldn't help it. Her head hurt. Had Taffy kicked her? Her left arm throbbed. Had her filly stepped on it?

Andi tried to move. Pain shot through her. She cried louder.

"Hush and keep still," a deep voice said.

Terror snatched away Andi's sobs. She gritted her teeth to keep her yells inside, but a whimper escaped.

"Aw, Pa, leave her be. She's hurtin' real bad. I think her arm's broke. Course she's gonna squall about it."

Sadie's worried voice broke through Andi's fear and pain. She opened her eyes.

Mr. Hollister held her in a tight grip on his horse. They were flying along at a swift gallop. Every time the horse's hooves hit the ground, pain stabbed Andi's arm.

New, scary thoughts popped into her head. *Why is Sadie's father here? Where is he taking me?* She caught her breath. *Where's Taffy? What happened?*

Andi looked around. Sadie galloped beside her on Jep. Taffy trailed behind, her reins clutched in Sadie's hand.

Slowly, the memory of what happened came back. The riding trick. Taffy taking off. Hitting the tree.

Her disobedience.

Warm drops trickled down Andi's face. They weren't tears. She lifted her good hand and wiped the drippy wetness away. Blood!

Andi's stomach turned over. She felt sick. A huge sob caught in her throat. She never imagined it would hurt so much not to obey.

Worse, the drumming hoofbeats were taking her farther and farther away from home.

"Let me go." Andi tried to wiggle out of Mr. Hollister's grasp. "I want my mother. I want to go home."

"Easy, gal," Mr. Hollister said. "I sent Zeke for your family. My place is closer. Granny will fix you up."

Granny? That scary old woman who'd scowled at Andi during the entire meal at the Hollisters? *No, no, no!*

Andi kicked and squirmed, setting her arm on fire. Her head pounded. She howled.

Mr. Hollister held her tighter. "Settle down."

Screaming didn't work. Neither did thrashing. It just wore Andi out and made her hurt worse. She went limp and let the tears roll down her cheeks. *I'm sorry, God. I'll never disobey again. Never, never, never!*

She gave in to the woozy, dizzy feeling and closed her eyes.

The next time Andi woke up, she was lying on a musty-smelling quilt in a dim room. A black ball of fur lay curled up beside her, purring. Only the white streak on his nose showed. Licorice!

Squeak. The bedsprings creaked.

Sadie crawled across the sagging mattress to Andi's side. "How do you feel?" She searched her face. "I didn't wanna leave you out there, but I had to fetch Pa. When we got back, you was lyin' so still that I thought . . ." Sadie swallowed. "I thought you was dead."

Andi stroked Licorice with her good hand. "I'm not dead, but I sure do hurt."

She looked around at the rough walls and one tiny window. The iron bed and a leaning wardrobe took up the whole space. "Where am I?"

"Ma and Pa's room." Sadie sat back. "Granny did a bang-up job on your arm. She's a healer. Knows every-thing about all kinds of herbs and medicines. Said it was an easy fix. You'll be good as new in a few weeks."

Andi's arm still throbbed, but not nearly so much as it had before. It lay at her side, splinted and wrapped tightly with strips of clean cloth. She touched her forehead. It was bandaged too and smelled of iodine.

"You got a goose egg from smashing into the tree," Sadie said. "You weren't used to doin' that trick like me and Zeke are. Your horse knew it." She bowed her head. "I'm sorry for gettin' you into this mess."

Fresh tears pooled in Andi's eyes. It wasn't Sadie's fault. "I knew I shouldn't do the trick," Andi said. "That's why I was so scared." She blinked. Teardrops ran down her cheeks and onto the faded quilt beneath her. "I want Mother."

Just then a large, work-worn hand drew aside the ragged curtain that served as a bedroom door. "She awake yet?" Mr. Hollister asked.

Before Sadie could answer, Chad ducked under the doorframe and pushed past Mr. Hollister. He rushed to Andi's side. His face looked pale under his tan. He shooed Sadie and the cat off the bed and took their place. "I came as fast as I could."

"Where's Mother?"

Chad shook his head. "She doesn't know about this yet. The Hollister boy—Zeke, I think—found me just the other side of your special spot." He smiled sadly. "I knew you were mad at me. I was on my way to see if you wanted to do a little fishing and talk about it."

Andi bit her lip. Mean, bossy Chad was being especially nice. Did he know about her disobeying?

"Zeke said you had a bad accident on Taffy." Chad reached out and gently stroked Andi's hair. "You can bet I pushed Sky to his fastest gallop to get here. I'm sorry. Taffy must be a little greener than I thought."

He gave Andi a puzzled frown. "Though I've never heard of you falling off a horse before. Very strange."

Nope. Chad didn't know.

He rose from the bed and lifted Andi into his arms. "Come on, little sister. Let's go home."

Andi wrapped her good arm around her brother's neck. "I want Mother."

Chad smiled. "I bet you do."

He carried Andi out of the dingy bedroom and into the main cabin. Half a dozen Hollisters stood around or sat on worn furniture, watching. Granny reclined in a rocking chair near the fireplace. Her bony hands gripped the armrests like an eagle's claws.

Mrs. Hollister stood next to the cookstove. "How 'bout a cup o' coffee before you go?"

Andi held her breath. Mr. Hollister and Chad were so angry at each other, it was a wonder her brother hadn't been shot when he rode up. Would he accept their hospitality?

Chad shook his head. "I really oughta get—"

"Please say yes," Andi whispered in his ear. "It's all right. I can stay a little longer."

Chad hesitated. He looked at Granny and the three little children hanging on her knees. He glanced at Mr. Hollister, who glared at him and shrugged. Finally, Chad smiled at Mrs. Hollister, carefully set Andi down on the bench, and removed his hat.

"Thank you, ma'am. Don't mind if I do."

CHAPTER 12

Good Neighbors

Chad settled himself next to Andi and put an arm around her. "I can't stay long. I need to get Andi home." He accepted the hot coffee with his free hand. "Thank you."

The next few minutes passed in awkward silence. Mrs. Hollister shuffled back and forth with coffee for her husband and Granny. Sadie snagged a cup for herself and sat down beside Andi. The little children, clearly bored, ran across the rough-plank floor and disappeared outside. Zeke vanished behind them.

The *creak, creak, creak* of Granny's rocking chair sounded loud in the stillness.

Mr. Hollister gulped down the last of his coffee. He crossed the room and dropped the tin cup in a dishpan. "I gotta get back to work."

Andi wondered if Mr. Hollister's work meant cutting up more of Chad's fence posts. There were a good many left in that long stretch of dried-up creek.

Chad shot up from the bench. "Hold on, Vince."

Mr. Hollister turned and bored Chad with a black look.

"If looks could kill, your brother would be dead right now," Sadie whispered in Andi's ear.

Andi didn't doubt it.

Chad crossed the room and stood in front of Mr. Hollister. "Vince, I . . . I'm grateful for what you did for my sister. You could have walked away. You didn't. We'll never see eye to eye on this boundary issue. We've exchanged enough threats and harsh words to start a range war, but I—"

"You got that right, boy," Mr. Hollister interrupted. He looked at Andi then back at Chad. "But that don't mean I'd leave a little child lyin' hurt and scared out on the range. What kind of man do you think I am?"

Andi knew what Chad thought of Mr. Hollister. Up until today, he was nothing more than a pesky neighbor who wanted to graze his sheep on Circle C rangeland.

Chad reddened, clearly uncomfortable with the question. He studied Mr. Hollister for a minute. Then he took a deep breath, as if his words needed help getting out. "I've changed my mind, Vince. We won't wait for the courts. I'll ask Justin to withdraw our case."

He paused. "The land is yours."

A pleased yelp came from Granny. Mrs. Hollister gasped and grabbed the counter for support. Sadie and Andi exchanged astonished looks.

Mr. Hollister gaped at Chad, speechless.

Chad stuck out his hand. "I don't intend to be your best friend, but I do want to be a good neighbor to someone who doesn't take out his personal grudges on the innocent. I was wrong about you, Vince. I'd like to show my thanks for what you did."

Slowly, as though he couldn't believe his ears, Mr. Hollister clasped Chad's outstretched hand. "I accept." Then he let go and stepped back. "Now, I'll thank you to pull out the rest of those fence posts, unless free firewood comes with the land."

Chad snorted. "I'll take care of it."

"Good."

"None of this means I like your sheep," Chad said. "You keep those walking vermin on your side of Spring Creek and off Circle C range, or there'll be real trouble. Folks say good fences make good neighbors, but that creek has always been fence enough for us." He grinned. "No matter where God decides to put it."

Vince laughed gruffly and agreed.

Chad scooped Andi up. "Let's get you home.

Mother will want Doc Weaver to take a look at your head and that arm."

"No need," Granny piped up from her rocker. "I tended her better than any doctor." She pushed out of her chair and joined the men. From her apron pocket she drew out a small brown bottle. "A swallow of this'll keep the child from hurtin' on the ride home."

Andi made a face but took the medicine.

Granny tucked the bottle away then poked Chad's belly with her cane. "I knew your pa when he first come out West. Never saw much of Jim Carter in you . . . until today." She gave him a wide, near-toothless smile.

Chad gently pushed the old woman's cane aside. "Thank you, ma'am."

He jammed his hat on his head, lifted Andi higher, and walked out of the Hollister cabin smiling.

꙳ ꙳

It was a long ride home. Andi fell asleep on Chad's lap listening to the *clip-clop* of Sky's hooves. Taffy followed behind on a lead rope.

Granny's medicine kept Andi asleep until she woke up in her own bed.

Mother smiled down at her. "I heard you had quite a day, sweetheart. I'm so sorry about your accident." Worry lines creased her forehead. "Chad feels terrible about it. He's trying to figure out where he went wrong with Taffy."

Andi's stomach flip-flopped.

"He blames himself for missing something. Taffy was supposed to be perfectly safe." Mother shook her head. "Chad's never been wrong about a horse before."

Andi's heart thumped so hard she thought for sure Mother would hear it. She had an awful choice: stay out of trouble by letting Chad think he'd missed something in Taffy's training, or confess her disobedience and take the punishment.

She cringed. Punishment was never fun.

An even worse thought came to mind. If Chad couldn't trust Taffy, then Andi would probably not be allowed to ride her alone. A broken arm would keep her off Taffy for several weeks, but keeping the truth to herself might keep Andi and Taffy apart for much, much longer.

What a terrible idea!

"There's nothing wrong with Taffy," she whispered tearfully. "It's my fault."

Slowly, word by word, Andi told the truth about what had happened. By the time she was finished, Mother held a sobbing Andi in her arms. Mother was crying too.

"I'm s-sorry," Andi choked out. "I was just so mad I didn't stop to think. When I finally did stop to think, it was too late. I bashed into the tree." She sniffed and hiccuped. "I promise I'll never, *ever* try another trick on Taffy without Chad's say-so."

Mother squeezed Andi tighter and forgave her. "I'm glad you told me the truth, sweetie. Chad wondered why Taffy would throw you, especially since you've never fallen off a horse on this ranch. He was truly puzzled."

"I know." Andi hiccuped and untangled herself from Mother's arms. She looked into her eyes. "Are you going to punish me?"

"Falling and breaking your arm is a much more painful reminder to obey than any punishment I could come up with."

Mother had a point. Andi remembered how much her head and arm hurt before Granny fixed her up.

"You also won't be riding Taffy for at least a month," Mother went on. "That seems like a natural but fitting punishment."

"Yes, ma'am." Andi rubbed her splinted arm. *A month is a long time.*

Mother sighed. "I do wish you didn't have to learn things the hard way. But sometimes, Andrea Rose, you are as hardheaded as your brother." She smiled and tapped Andi's nose.

Andi hiccuped again. "Which one?"

Mother laughed. "Chad, of course."

At that moment, a certain big brother strolled into Andi's room. "Did I hear my name just now?"

"You most certainly did." Mother rose from the bed and motioned Chad over. "I have supper to manage, so I will leave you two alone. You have a lot to talk about."

Chad's eyebrows rose. He looked at Andi. "We do?"

Andi smiled at her mother then turned back to Chad. "We sure do." She patted the bed. "Sit down, big brother. I'm going to tell you everything."

And she did.

History Fun
Sheep and Cattle Wars

Andi's brothers are cattlemen. They don't like sheep. Chad calls them "walking, stinking vermin," which means he thinks of them as pests. Andi has heard all her life how sheep destroy grazing land. They could strip a valley clean of all grass. Some cowboys insisted sheep stank so badly that cattle wouldn't graze wherever sheep had been. Sheep were also accused of ruining the watering holes so the cattle couldn't drink there.

That makes a good story, but is it really true? Were sheep as bad as the cattlemen said? Partly true. Partly not true. It depends on who is telling the story—the sheepherders or the cattlemen.

Most of the arguments broke out because of something called "open range." This meant nobody owned the land and everybody could use it. In the 1800s, cattlemen were the kings of the West. They had a we-were-here-first attitude and did not want to share the open range with sheep, for the reasons mentioned above.

While it is true sheep can eat the grass until the land is stripped bare, there was plenty of land to go around—thousands of acres. In fact, some ranchers raised cattle and sheep together.

It was only a small number of cattlemen who couldn't get along with their sheep-raising neighbors. These sheepherders and cattlemen fought each other for fifty years in several states. The cattlemen always did the attacking. During those fifty years, 53,000 sheep, twenty-eight sheepherders, and sixteen cowboys lost their lives because of this deadly disagreement.

Toward the end of the 1800s, ranchers and sheepherders began to fence their private property. Open range became a thing of the past. Since the cattle and sheep no longer grazed together, the wars came to an end. Everybody raised whatever animals they chose within their own fences.

"Good fences make good neighbors" proved to be the best thing that ever happened for the cattlemen and sheepherders of the Old West.

**For more Andi fun,
download free activity pages
at CircleCSteppingStones.com.**

Susan K. Marlow is always on the lookout for a new story, whether she's writing books, teaching writing workshops, or sharing what she's learned as a homeschooling mom. Susan is the author of several series set in the Old West—ranging from new reader to young adult—and she enjoys relaxing on her fourteen-acre homestead in the great state of Washington. Connect with the author at CircleCSteppingStones.com or by emailing Susan at SusanKMarlow@kregel.com.

Leslie Gammelgaard, illustrator of the Circle C Beginnings and Circle C Stepping Stones series, lives in beautiful Washington state where every season delights the senses. Along with illustrating books, Leslie inspires little people (especially her four grandchildren) to explore and express their creative nature through art and writing.

Grow Up with Andi!

Don't miss any of Andi's adventures in the
Circle C Beginnings series

Andi's Pony Trouble
Andi's Indian Summer
Andi's Fair Surprise
Andi's Scary School Days
Andi's Lonely Little Foal
Andi's Circle C Christmas

For readers ages 9–13!

Andi's adventures continue in the Circle C Adventures series

Andrea Carter and the Long Ride Home
Andrea Carter and the Dangerous Decision
Andrea Carter and the Family Secret
Andrea Carter and the San Francisco Smugglers
Andrea Carter and the Trouble with Treasure
Andrea Carter and the Price of Truth

**Free enrichment activities are available at
CircleCAdventures.com.**